Outdoor Opposites

Written by Brenda Williams · Illustrated by Rachel Oldfield

Sung by The Flannery Brothers

Barefoot Books

step inside a story

I can stand up,

or I can
sit down.

I can smile,

or I can frown.

I can run,

or I can walk.

I can listen,

or I can...

talk!

I am doing opposites.

High!

Low!

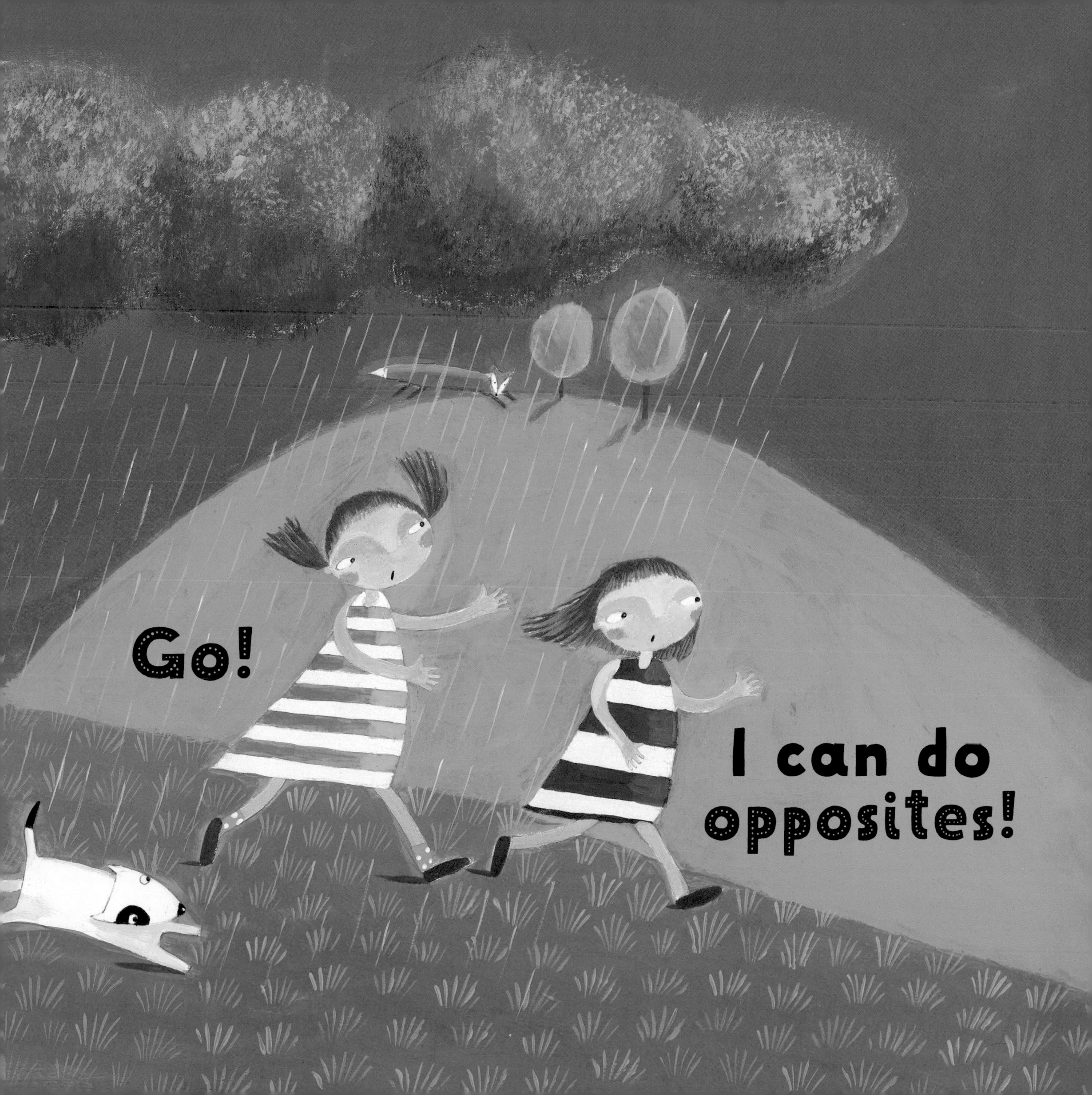

Go!

I can do opposites!

I can
whisper,

or I can...

or I can jump OUT.

I can
taste good
things,

or I can
taste bad.

Show!

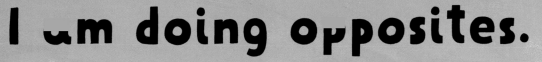

I am doing opposites.

I can do
opposites!

Outdoor Opposites

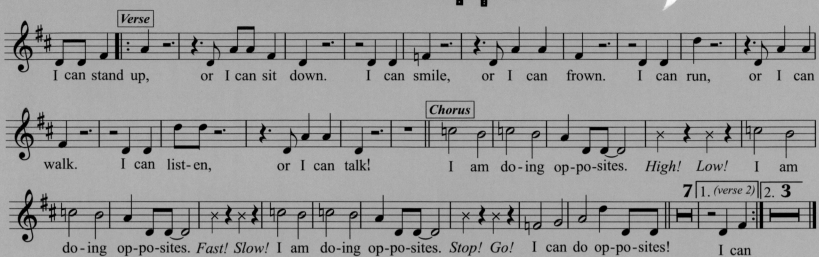

Verse

I can stand up, or I can sit down. I can smile, or I can frown. I can run, or I can walk. I can list-en, or I can talk!

Chorus

I am do-ing op-po-sites. *High! Low!* I am do-ing op-po-sites. *Fast! Slow!* I am do-ing op-po-sites. *Stop! Go!* I can do op-po-sites!

1. (verse 2) 2. 3 I can

Barefoot Books • 2067 Massachusetts Ave • Cambridge • MA 02140 • Barefoot Books • 29/30 Fitzroy Square • London • W1T 6LQ

Text copyright © 2015 by Brenda Williams. Illustrations copyright © 2015 by Rachel Oldfield. The moral rights of Brenda Williams and Rachel Oldfield have been asserted. Musical composition copyright © 2015 by Sam Dixon. This arrangement by The Flannery Brothers
Music performed by Dan and Mike Flannery. Backing vocals by Nick DeRosa and Third Street Music Settlement Preschool; piano recorded at RetroMedia Studios, Red Bank, New Jersey; drums performed by Andrew Clifford, Main Street Music Studios, Bangor, Maine.
Recorded, mixed and mastered by Jumping Giant, New York City
Animation by Sophie Marsh, Sarita McNeil and Lauren Fitzpatrick, Bristol, UK

First published in the United States of America by Barefoot Books, Inc
and in Great Britain by Barefoot Books, Ltd in 2015
The paperback edition with enhanced CD first published in 2015
All rights reserved

Graphic design by Katie Jennings Campbell, Asheville, NC, USA
Reproduction by Bright Arts (HK) Ltd, Hong Kong
Printed in China on 100% acid-free paper
This book was typeset in Mr. Anteater, Mr. Lucky, and Mrs. Lollipop
The illustrations were prepared in acrylics

Hardback with enhanced CD ISBN 978-1-78285-094-6
Paperback with enhanced CD ISBN 978-1-78285-095-3

British Cataloguing-in-Publication Data: a catalogue
record for this book is available from the
British Library. Library of Congress
Cataloging-in-Publication Data
is available upon request

7 9 8

Go to **www.barefootbooks.com/opposites**
to access your audio singalong
and video animation online.